Skreet:
A Fable of Ink & Influence

Alia-Enor Bath and Basil Psanoudakis

AOS Publishing, 2025

ISBN: 978-1-998662-69-2

Cover Design: Basil Psanoudakis

Visit AOS Publishing's website:
www.aospublishing.com

Don't Silence the Story Tellers

1

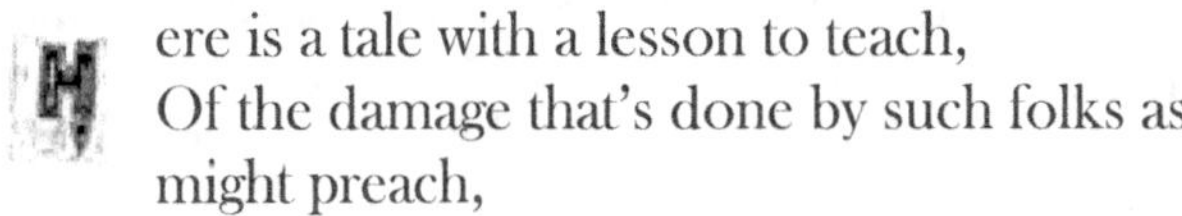ere is a tale with a lesson to teach,
Of the damage that's done by such folks as
might preach,
From a creed that they rate above figurative speech –
And what happens when dreams become over-reach.

The events that unfold, as the minstrels declaim,
An apocryphal tale of truth, loyalty, and fame,
That cannot be proven, for a fable's a trade-off;
Between history and rhyme – it's not lies we're afraid
of.

A primitive land of green pastures and castles,
Besmirched by its peasants, their lords, and some
vassals.

The richest ran rackets that kept the low-born
Eking a living on ears of corn and
Drinking their rot-gut in huts made from cow pats,
While townsfolk fled soldiers with short swords and
tin hats.

For the law of the land offered extra-harsh justice
For telling a lie: A madness the reckless
Would seldom dare try, lest they're caught in the
deed.
A gibbet's no home if you've family to feed.

Though soldiers might seem the least likely to fact-
check,
Their bosses were tossers who knew where the truth's
kept;
Proving a falschood would work on the precept
That no truth existed unprinted in codec.

Up in that grand hall, a Press turned apace,
Printing out pages of all that took place.
Its inventor, our hero, worked night and day,
So his people could progress beyond their melee;
... It was his quest, you might say.

His press printed truth, and nothing else but,
By magic was fact-driven litho-cut:
Which crops to plant, the time of the sunrise,
The path of a messenger, tallied supplies.

Everything was whisked up, the facts of this world,
Stamped out onto sheets as the reams were unfurled,
Then rolled or bound,
The tomes were stacked,
The scrolls in boxes,
The boxes in racks –
Each fact exact.

Of the man who spent all of his days locked away,
Spacing his ligatures, inking his trays,
Of Skreet we could say:

Skreet was a pencilhead born to a castle,
Who dreamed of expanding his powers to marshal
The rabble he ruled, as their need to be schooled
Was good luck for the leader least likely to be
fooled.

His skin was as vellum, his hair was as ink;
His forehead was vast, for he'd vast things to think.
His thoughts were superior in every way.
To anything anyone else thought to say.

Never doubt the honesty of his motivation;
It couldn't be that fame, or world domination,
In any way informed his operation.
If he thought briefly on adoration,
The explanation was his orientation,
For who does not find titillation
In all forms of written communication?

His ambition, if ever you asked him the question,
Would be to spread truth. Skreet: Man with a
Vision!

2

 Market day, Skreet's citadel bustles and
steams,
At full crank, the printer dispatches live-streams.
The town's finance alone could be measured in
reams,
As leaf after sheaf spewed from the machine.

The sound was a clamour, a whirring and clatter,
And somewhere above that, excited chatter.
Skreet paused his routine: 'Voices? What could be
the matter?'

For all kinds of nuisance, his court room has uses;
His subjects and soldiers, the unwashed he indulges,
Could seek out his guidance, though they seldom
would dare.
Events he need manage were brought to him there.

Guards armed with cutlass, dozens in surplus,
Had dragged in a young maid, whose sweetness
delicious
Seemed meek and defenceless in all of this ruckus.
Skreet went down to survey this circus's purpose.

They were crowded around her, they caused her to
kneel;
Skreet couldn't see what had inspired such zeal.
She was simply quite charming. Douyin started his
spiel ...

Douyin was Skreet's right-hand man.
Righteous, reliable, efficient, invariable,
A long-term associate of untold value.
Almost a friend. Confirmed partisan.

Where Skreet's time was consumed in capturing
language,
Trustworthy Douyin was off-stage to manage
The comings and goings, the to-ings and fro-ings
Of guards and of farmers, with jail times and sowings.

Douyin drew himself up like a hot air balloon,
And started the tale of his glorious platoon,
Who'd marched through the town square from
morning to noon,
To keep all in order, to protect Skreet's fortune.

Skreet gestured to Douyin. 'Is the point coming
soon?'

And while he was speaking, the young lady kept
peeking
At Skreet and the citadel that was his for safe-
keeping,
As though she were dreaming of sleeping and eating,
Not treating this meeting as the prequel to beatings.

With pompous officiousness, Douyin huffed a sigh,
'This bard, in public, we caught singing a lie.'
The story, it transpired, (bold-print face, thick red
dye)
Was the tale of Lala-Lai, famed peddler of 'they
say...'
A minstrel whose bread was what she could play.

Lala-Lai: A creative,
Her face was her talent,
A minstrel, a singer,
Renowned Influencer.
Adore her, envy her,
It's not free to see her;
She's yours for a payment –
Four easy instalments.

A slip of a thing, her smile was pert,
Her instrument plucky; her face was a flirt.

And though she knelt, she was not deferential.
She caught Skreet's eye, admired his big pencil.

He puffed up with pride, at her blush and her swoon,
Overcome by his paper dust and ink-stained
costume.

Douyin was a doer of practical things,
Not swayed by her features, his face remained grim.
Into the silence, he repeated her sin:
'She was singing a lie!' The young lady grinned.

'What song was it?' Skreet wanted to know,
For a small-scale offence he might soften his blow.

'I sang a romance, a heart-felt tale,
How the lord of this manor loved a travelling
female'.
She fluttered her veil.

Skreet knew nothing of singers, and not much of
songs,
But felt disinclined to punish her wrongs.

Her smile was a hook. Douyin gave him a look.
'She told a tale not printed in the book!'

Demurely, the vixen's sweet chin tilted up.
'I made it up.'

Chapter and verse, taboo and worse,
Who would admit to a crime so cursed?

'You lied?' She nodded, while Douyin, swollen-
headed,
Mandated a ruling she ought to have dreaded.

'Seven years!' was his verdict, predictably strict,
And the court cheered on loudly, inflamed to
convict.

Skreet could not disagree; he gave the decree,
'Seven years' servitude, with enforced honesty!'

If a moment's remorse overcame him,
At a life so foreshortened, her passions thwarted,
Skreet doubted the feeling was very important.

'What could convince such a sweet maid to do it?'

Fame and fortune, love and attention,
A roof and a kitchen instead of abstention.
Lala-Lai would not admit that,
Cream-gotten kitty cat,
'Perhaps you would help me improve my
intentions?'

'I might, at that.'

Douyin smiled without pleasure.

A guard spat.

3

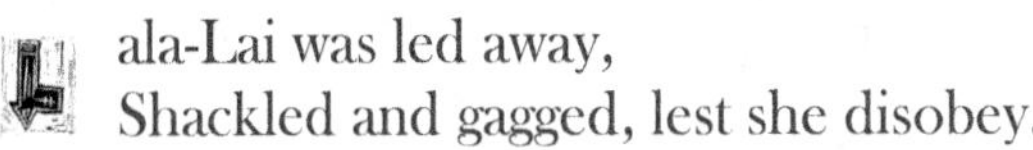 ala-Lai was led away,
Shackled and gagged, lest she disobey.

Douyin was tasked with the final binding,
More gentle than flaying,
Preventing her saying
more lies,
or dismaying the wise.
Stern as fixed type-face, he kept her apprised:
'Terms and conditions apply.'

Lala-Lai, in her distress, kneeling before the printing
press,
Felt her words repressed, without egress.

His droning voice
Dispelled her choice.
What was in her head
Must be proof-read.

She may not utter a thought unfettered
That's not first printed, and from there vetted.

'If I deem your scripting fair,
Your words are yours, for you to share.
But if your words are found untrue,
Your punishment, of course, falls due.'

His spell landed
Heavy-handed.
Her head sagged.
He removed her gag.

The blocks lined up between their stays;
The crank turned,
The pages churned,
A small and mewling word discerned.

One lowercase eye,
its sequel letter kicking high.

He nodded and passed her the page:
'OK,' it stated.
She voiced it. 'OK.'

Pencilhead Skreet was moodily brooding,
Jealousy looping, opposing thoughts feuding.

On the one hand, in Skreet, Lala-Lai's features
kindled
A new-found desire like a sizzling tingle;

And yet on the other, he knew that her stories
Had gone and garnered her *his* due glory.

She'd stolen his limelight, his cheering ovation,
Just as he'd planned to seek adulation.

She'd journaled such lies, scribbled such drivel;
She'd frivolled his laurels, and trampled his marvel.

Lala-Lai's wit had sparkled, her features bedazzled;
No wonder his townsfolk had ogled, befuddled.

Just an innocent herald who'd been over-persuaded,
She'd learn to be better if she was regulated.

He'd guide her; she'd honour his brilliance
unrivalled,
And maybe in time she would meet his high
scruples.

Skreet's weaselling thoughts circled, snarled, and
entangled.
For now she was muzzled, her jingles were strangled.
Her vocals he'd cudgelled; Lala-Lai would be
cancelled.

Come morning, the tumult of clamorous thoughts
Had thinned to a duel of opposing reports.

One was: though she's sweet,
Lala-Lai might just keep.
He couldn't afford a distraction right now.

For the other: Skreet knew
He must plan his debut –
His world domination started now.

In the pre-dawn light, he packed for his flight:
His robes, his fortunes, his entitlement, his Rights,
And his wondrous tome that had printed overnight.

Parchment stamped with inky smear.
The world would do well to hear
The words of Skreet, Truth Engineer.

And as to the path he'd plotted to tread,
He'd follow her own steps in retrospect,
Undoing her words in each place they'd been said.

His people would recognise his unequalled lore;
At each stage of his journey, his press would print
more.

The display that he'd make to towns far and wide
Would bedazzle the dim and awe-strike the wise.

Yes, she was fair and beautifully dressed,
Clutching her lute to her bounteous breast.

But Skreet peddled truth, not improper verse –
His people would love him, or learn what was worse.

He'd spent years in his high tower, turning the
wheels,
While phonies and fibbers were cooling their heels,
And the honour that was due him bedecked
imbeciles.

Douyin could manage here, that was the deal.

4

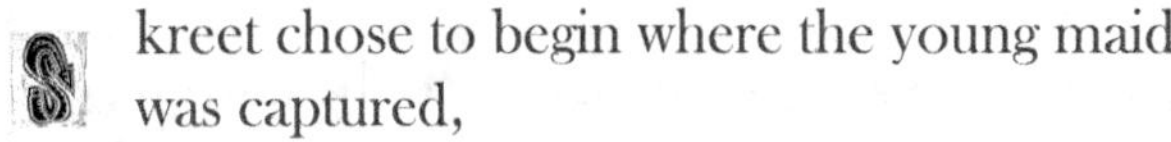 kreet chose to begin where the young maid
was captured,
Assured he would have his own people enraptured.

He'd undo her wrongdoing, and make good through
his lecture,
Compounding his prize as his peasants learned
culture.

On cobbled lanes beneath his own castle,
His tome as his pulpit, he read from the missal
Such truths of this town, as his own book could tell,
Though the verse of his sermon didn't mention the
smell.
...And oration was hard when all else was pell-mell.

Folks lived on the streets and shat in the alleyways,
Infected the wells with dead cats on the holy-days.

While up above, parchment drifted the currents,
Below teemed, overcrowded, with music discordant,
Sufficient to out chime his own aggrandisement.

Peasants and servants, allegiant in pageant,
Bore torrents of parchment, like pennants
resplendent,
Fomenting a penchant for riotous excitement,
Too booming and clamorous withal for
enlightenment.

Bemired little minds, resisting his system,
Would listen to pop songs yet disdain his wisdom.

Except for two beggars, dressed mostly in rags,
Who'd built up a fireplace and laid out their swags,
Proposing to preachers, or pilfering bags.

Skreet's voice had grown hoarse from attempting discourse,
His sermon and soapbox a neglected resource.

So when these philosophers, wise men or cracked,
Offered a place to him, he thankfully sat.

Poets, the two of them, one deaf and one blind,
Burning up pages, speaking their mind.

Skreet listened to all of the words as they tumbled,
Jugglers with concepts too wordy, too mumbled.

Did anything they spoke of come to pass?
Was the measure of wisdom a pain in his arse?
Would his truth ever be uttered in this scattered
word-farce?
Was he here as a teacher, or just part of the class?
Speaking in tongues, he at least thought they'd ask.

Eventually Skreet showed them his wondrous book,
And laid down some hard facts: the truth that it took.

The blind one read nothing, the deaf one spoke less.
Were they wise when they offered this piece of
advice:

'You cannot force people to seek out the truth.
Loyalty wants flattery, it's almost fool-proof.
Fame is awaiting you under your roof'

They followed this wisdom with slanging forsooth:
A beat poem, rhyme-busting, snaggle-toothed.
And their fire crackled merrily, fuelled by his truth.

Meanwhile, in the Citadel, Douyin's charge was
print-bound,
As he taught her the gear she must operate now.
Lala-Lai's wily ways kept her jailor around.

In the depths of the press the gears were all kept,
Clean and neat, and frequently swept.
The job she fulfilled? To top-up the ink wells,
To burnish the plates, and mop up any spills.

At the end of the day, Douyin led her away,
And fed her and found her somewhere to lay.

So tired, her head ached from a day's worth of
clatter,
Yet her lips remained sealed against idle chatter.

On day two Douyin fetched her for further hard
work,
And he smiled, all unwieldy, in the absence of talk.

She reached for her brushes, the mops, and the rags,
Her hair in a tangle, cheeks smudged, shoulders
sagged.

And that day, her own words as yet unuttered,
She completed her work with her friendliness
shuttered.

She needed to wash, but another day passed
Before she dare ask for the path to the bath.

Douyin blushed, and set someone else to the task,
Eyeing with envy the servant he'd asked.

But later, printed paper gave word of her thanks –
the first time she'd spoken. One page: mostly blank.

Her days might seem endless, but they were still few.
When the smiles that he sent her were returned, as
his due,
And Douyin began to admire the view.
... She knew it, too.

And after a while, he learned of her thoughts,
For the things she was thinking he'd sought to court.
He considered them truthful, the things she'd report.

He read every word that she'd think of to say:
That he was strong and discerning, that he was
leading the way,
And none of them seemed to him lies – so they'd
stay.

Her goal had adjusted, a new net had been cast.
Offended when Skreet left, but thinking fast,
Douyin was still better than hanging bare-assed.

The more that she flattered him, the more he
believed,
And the more that she used the truth to deceive.

Sitting by Douyin for the evening repast,
She'd mentioned his nature, his skill-set so vast,
And damned if those pages didn't print fast.
Not that she'd test it, but her speed-tests all passed.

She'd spoken to liken his profile to nobles,
And the page fully-throttled, arrived on the double.

She remarked that his family had raised a fine son,
And the words almost sounded before she'd begun.

For Skreet on his journey, a prodigious occurrence.
A burgeoning increase inflating print's furtherance.
The book had expanded beyond all known
precedents,
Which Skreet took to be a progressive development.

How could he know that Lala-Lai had learned a new
trick,
To get her words printed, and the printed words
ticked;

In the midst of his lecture, a few pages more,
Unheeded by yokels, slid to the floor.

They said: 'Douyin, Your eyes are so keen.
'How has your wisdom remained unseen?'

Other phrases, sweet and flirtatious,
Appearing on pages which Skreet found vexatious,
Especially the most injurious of all:
'The glory built here reflects on *you* more'.
Skreet could barely lift the thing.
His head sharpened pointwise, like his book:
expanding.
He'd best hasten his fame, before troubles arose,
Without him to manage his servants' egos

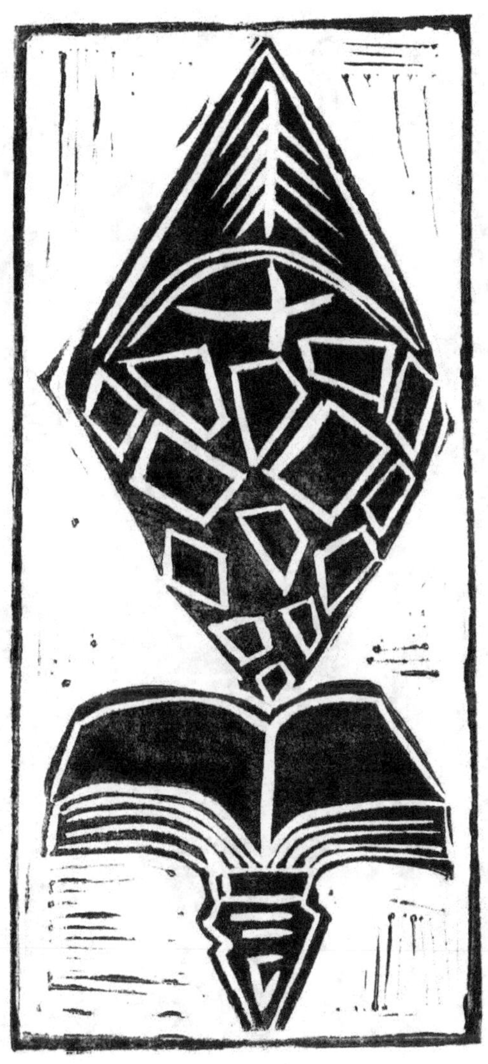

5

hat night, by lamplight, Skreet plotted his next
site.
He need not court hicks who he owned as his
birthright;
He'd gain more from a town that would trade for his
insight.
He slept, and his tome grew a chapter by first light.

On his next day he took to the road with a troupe,
And they smiled as he read them his tales for their
soup.

They ignored his recital of measures and scales,
But when he told of the marriages, births, and
betrayals,
They paid him in kind with embellished details.

When at the next town he prepared a new stage,
His tome grew again as he opened the page.

Scene two; exterior; the neighbour's town square,
Common folks showed him no more respect there.
Amid pastries, glass jewels, and the theatre troupe,
Skreet's smarts fell like farts in a chicken coop.

As his show of great wisdom failed to attract,
Skreet pondered new targets to aim at with facts.

Perhaps the bureaucrats?
Whoever wrote the farmer's almanacs?

His tome was a podium, a glorious display,
Yet somehow the masses could still look away.
He spruiked his wares,
But garnered few stares,
Dim-witted rustics preferring hearsay.

At home Lala-Lai was testing her sway,
with an innocent play to go out for the day.
When her sweet words were heard, she'd learned
what to say.

Her 'esteem for Douyin could not be feigned'
He was 'stronger and wiser than everyone claimed',
She felt that his 'management was over-constrained'.
Douyin was being trained.

Easy enough, then, to ask him a favour:
She'd been working so hard, he'd never nay-say her.
That was how Lala-Lai left The Press for a day,
and meandered and day-dreamed along streets and
by-ways.

She dared not speak much, for drawing attention.
If Douyin was busy, he'd thank her abstention.
It wasn't about secrets, but reprieve from detention.

Voiceless, she found her smiles abound –
coy glances at minstrels, despite their vile sound.
She curtseyed at nurses, and nuns spitting curses,
meandered past vendors, esteemed money-lenders.

Until, at the lowest part of the town,
On a grotty patch of cobbled ground,
She found two beggars, who spent their day
burning the pages that floated their way.

One was dumb, both were grey;
the sightless one had much to say,
Beginning with an exclamation: 'Lala-Lai!'

She mimed out her tale, and while one watched
intently,
the other foretold of bad omens aplenty.

'The blind won't read' – she'd listened to this
prophesy.
'The deaf don't hear;
fame is what you need;
the future has no history'
'Truth or lies, they both burn bright,' said the blind
to the speechless,
and Lala-Lai left for the night.

6

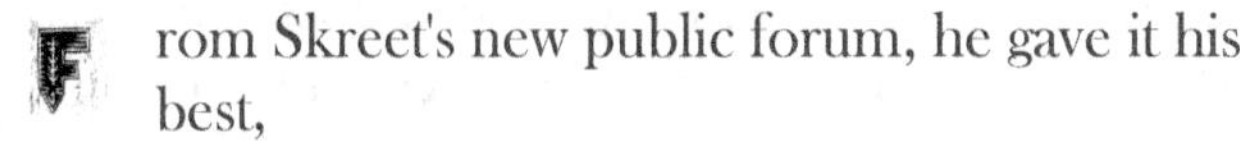

From Skreet's new public forum, he gave it his
    best,
But found that the crowd here still couldn't care less.
Attempting to wow them, he leafed through new text,
For surely they'd value the news that came next?

On its axis the planet had turned, as expected;
Egg prices were up, a new statue erected,
a gentleman's offer was duly accepted.

And one final page that detailed the journey,
Lala-Lai walked the town streets all smiling and flirty,
And probably fibbing to bumpkins below.
Had Douyin allowed this? Unchaperoned? No!

Though Skreet's passions ran high, his temper's
untried,
He thought himself gentle, considered, perhaps wise.
So whence came this murderous look in his eyes?
His head swelled in size.
He tore that one page in his white-knuckled fist,
Packed up his wherewithal, red-faced and tight-
lipped,

Envisioning shrieking, perhaps a good beating,
At the least that girl's punishment would need some
tweaking.
Best hire a cart, leave this swill to their parts,
And trundle his book back to the start.

He hunted down Douyin for a serious talk.
'Faithful,' he spat to himself as he stalked.

Douyin, who was working deep in the archives,
was caught by surprise when his master arrived.

There was no pre-amble –
Skreet yelled; Douyin scrambled.

'I expected a jailor and not a tour guide.'
To Skreet's opening salvo, Douyin internally sighed.

'So how many times did she get her way?'
Skreet asked, but his servant had nothing to say.

Skreet's pencilhead grew as his mild manners
slipped.
He re-asked his question but altered the script.

'Had she tried to escape the terms of her stay?'
Douyin answered: he'd been with her for most of
every day.

'Had she led Douyin on to gain favour, did he
think?'
Douyin said that he doubted he'd fall for that trick.

Holding his ground, Douyin carefully ventured:
'Skreet, are you jealous?' then prepared to be
lectured.

Skreet's temperature rose with his bottled-up
rancour,
But punitive measures worked as treatment for
anger.

He gestured towards the printing press hall.
'No one shall enter, nor leave from these walls!'

Douyin's jaw dropped, but his response was stopped
by Skreet's final: 'That is all.'

And Skreet flounced off in a fit of harsh justice,
while Douyin was left to arrange bricks and mortice.

Thus the windows were sealed and the exits, bar one,
were lost to stone-masons. No more air, no more sun,
leaving Lala-Lai to ponder what she had done.

You Can Sing for Me

7

The matter thus settled, Skreet's poise was
    regained,
Leaving him eager to resume his campaign.

So he slept by his press, and when he awoke,
with the sun's early rising, when the first sparrows
spoke,
he made his way down to his obtuse homefolk.
At her breakfast, sweet silent Lala-Lai sat,
from the windows above, the printing press spat:
'sparrows *sing*'.
      Not that anyone read that.

Skreet's second departure ran as well as the first.
He gathered his baggage, his tasks were dispersed.
Douyin nodded to everything, obedient and terse.

Skreet spent that day in a crowded tavern,
Tempting in henchmen with roast meats and a
flagon.

How else to sway fools with his superior worth?
Coercion would work best on such barren earth.
So with soldiers of fortune, and weapons to spare,
His troupe made their way to a new market square,
Intending to force some respect from crowds there.

His tome held aloft, almost bursting its bindings.
The flourishing text grew like lightning striking.

The lectern groaned under the great book's sheer
size,
But even at sword-point, crowds failed to eulogise.

For his part, Douyin had requested respectfully
His charge use all caution, avoid further hostility,
As Skreet's toxic brutality could hurt her
immeasurably.

She blushed in response, his first compliment to her.
Her investment's return, the success of her lure,
and now how to punish an evil wrong-doer ...
Vindictive?   So sue her.

Lala-Lai asked her warder:
'Perhaps there's a way I might stay in my quarters,
without tethers or tortures to keep me in order.'

Douyin would help her, however he may,
Since Skreet doubted him anyway.

'My songs have gone silent without me to sing them,
'But why suppress that which involves no deception?

'Is there no way, despite this tale's villain,
'To let music be free, outside of my prison?'

Douyin read her request and read it again.
If she could not escape, then what could she mean?

'I mean for your talent to spread my word wide,
without breaking the rules that your master applied.

'You can sing for me.' Lala-Lai's eyes were wide.
'I'll be your guide.'

Douyin's talent for the musical craft was slight,
Yet he learned her first song on that very first night –
reciting in verse the tale of her plight.

He knew the real story, did Douyin the wise;
he'd been there himself, this verse held no lies.

The tune was not new, but was borrowed a little,
the borrowing subtle, a jingle to whistle.
Her lyrics, more lyrical than the boring original,
would likely go viral if Douyin was amenable.
(He wasn't unusable.)

She instructed his postures, his gestures, his suit,
Rehearsed him 'till finger-tips bled on her lute.
And then she explained where he should go to sing:
The usual assembly for minstrels cribbing.

A mid-career comeback for Lala-Lai,
who knew all about making enemies pay.

And her 'mentor' Douyin, that man was a trip.
She'd break, for his sake, his loyalty to his lordship,
and protect her place by furthering their courtship.

She was satisfied when, at the end of the day,
As she left for her bed, he asked her to stay.

For his part, in the dark Douyin lay,
not thinking of singing, nor the commitments he'd
made.
His brain was too coddled with thoughts of Lala-Lai.

Her sweet smile, gentle, sunny,
fingers brushing, heartbeat bumping,
Consequences were too complex.
Lulling dreams, heaving swelling,
Douyin was dwelling on thoughts of Lala-Lai.

Skreet; A Fable of Ink & Influence
You Can Sing for Me

8

 n every town square Skreet had carried his
book;
He'd been out-shouted by players and their
gobbledygook,
and the songs of the minstrels with superior looks.
He was too proud to sook.

He was told by two beggars, 'folks won't seek the
truth.'
And the soldiers he'd hired had not helped spread
his news.
He'd need simpler text to induce reasoned views;
These townsfolk were clearly too easily confused.

To help them, he removed a few sheets from his
book;
Refining the text might help garner a look,
A line here or there was all that it took –
It wasn't cheating, just baiting the hook.

Then on the street corner he heard a new tune,
and the words they were crooning had all the crowd
swooning.
(Although all Skreet could hear was Douyin's road to
ruin.)

Of a minstrel, her sponsor, and the songs that they
shared;
their hardships, their triumphs, and how they now
fared,

But surely that ditty was Lala-Lai's history, including
the tales of Douyin?

Pity him, you can't save his skin!

At home Lala-Lai
wrote songs every day
for Douyin to play.

And her words were mostly true,
when framed as just her view,
with only minor hints and clues
About Skreet and how he behaved.

And when Douyin sang her tunes,
convinced he was to lies immune,
The songs rang true; though in part that's due
to Douyin's so-called impartial view.

All the while in the citadel,
as each new night fell,
and the press rolled out page after page,
the press-hall was choking
on the sheets that kept spilling,
which were blocked from escaping;
so the room, slowly filling,
had the occupants swimming
in the tales of Lala-Lai.

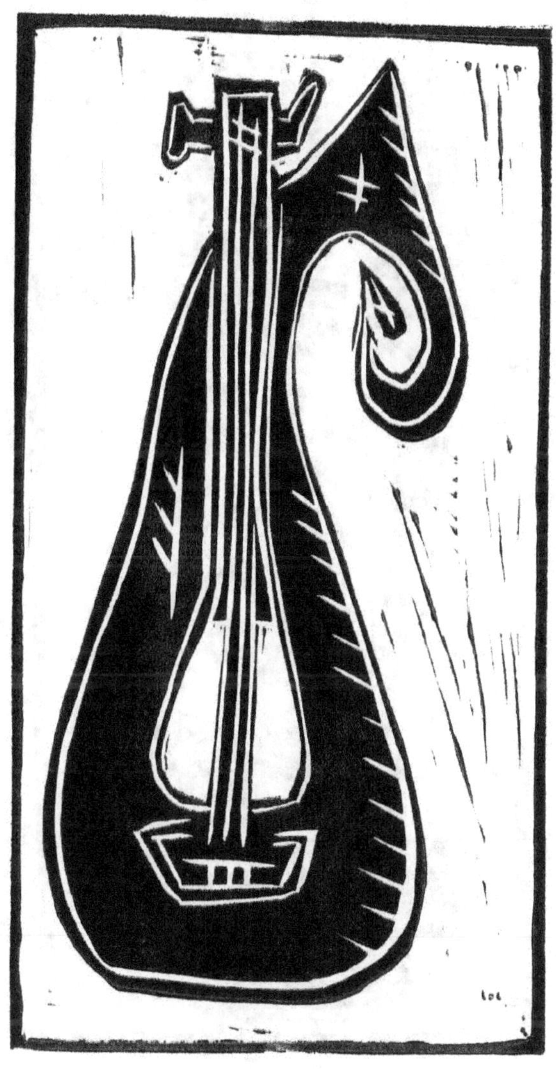

9

kreet returned home like a storm after calm,
    Stomped into his hall where the light was dim,
and printed sheets
in stacks and heaps,
filled the rooms up to the brim –
nothing escaped, nothing came in.

Except for the apostate Douyin.
Who knew that that bastard could sing?

The two lovebirds were flirting in the darkened
press-hall,
With a lute on their laps and a trapped caterwaul,
Echoing verse Skreet did not like at all.
It made his skin crawl.

Skreet should be hero,
not this hustling by-blow,
and the drivel she peddled to disloyal Douyin.

They froze when they saw him,
which gave him the opening:
'I silenced her, you let her sing?
I should tear you from limb to limb!'

Skreet fumed,
his pencil grew.
Tension bloomed

...Until Lala-Lai excused:
'I've done nothing taboo.'
So the printed page stated,
from a press he'd created
for truth...

      ... unplacated,
Skreet's pencil inflated.
To the dungeon they were fated.

'Speak fast if you think you can save your skin.'
Skreet's anger was sustaining him.

'With my hand on my heart, these words I speak are
true.'

Lala-Lai looked sincere,
like she held her truth dear:

'There is no greater value your people see in you
Than the pages which from your printing press
issue.'

True enough, as the beggars had shown
by burning the pages to keep themselves warm.

'And there is no greater loyalty a man could display
Than the loyalty Douyin has shown.'

If his loyalty was to her, they did not let that be
known.

"To set you at ease, I'll say one final thing;
Since living here, I don't have that urge to sing.'

Why would she? Her songs flourished, thanks to
Douyin.

Skreet's anger abated, for a moment at least,
though still aggravated by the green-eyed beast.

Then just as he dropped the last page of her script,
The press juddered again, and another page slipped,
And he read that too – it was the daily manuscript.

'In the citadel, a tyrant who tells lies but seeks praise,
Is threatening violence to more talented maids.'

White-lipped, Skreet flipped.

Lala-Lai snorted, mocking Skreet's shocked face.
'Who dared print this disgrace?'
Skreet pointed her way. 'You've corrupted this
place.'
Douyin entered the fray. 'We print only the truth, or
am I off-base?'

'The truth!' Skreet bellowed,
Confused fellow.
Angry because
either the press was at fault, or he was.

Then to beat his bruised
ego
was Lala-Lai's salvo:
'Your pencilhead's
hollow,
Your ambition is nutso;
I'd back my own songs
over any 'truth' you know.'

Skreet shook with fierce
aggro,
attempted to land blows
and failed, to his sorrow.

Lala-Lai backed away.
Douyin tried to follow,
Then tripped by print
strewn,
as Skreet fed his own
ruin,
by breaking the lute
to silence the tune.
His press wasn't immune.

Gears ground in homage
To cat-gut sabotage,
Pages jammed stages,
in inch-thick découpage.

The printing press
grumbled,
It gears bungled,
resulting in jumbles
as stacked pages tumbled,
until the hall rumbled.
The three quarrellers
stumbled,
foundations mangled
as fresh masonry
crumbled.

Skreet's temple in
shambles,
Life's work disassembled.

On the streets below, two beggars watched
as the citadel tumbled and the townsfolk were squashed,
And everywhere scrambled, fearful and lost, the great unwashed.

Skreet's ambition succeeded in this one small way:
He'd go down in history for this calamitous day,
A song generations of minstrels would play.
And Douyin the loyal, of whom they would say:
'You thought Donkeys could bray.'

And assuming our song-bird, from her gilded cage flew,
She failed her ambition, but we'll give this review:
She was more honest than all of them, at least this she knew:
'To your own self be true.'

Rich man, poor man, truth-teller, priest,
Ambition's the same for every beast;
They'll still hunger for love after a feast,
And where hunger's thwarted, truth is unleashed.
Failure to grasp this was the downfall of Skreet.

9 781998 662692